Richard Duane

A memorial of Nathan B. Crocker, D.D.

Richard Duane

A memorial of Nathan B. Crocker, D.D.

ISBN/EAN: 9783337260156

Printed in Europe, USA, Canada, Australia, Japan

Cover: Foto ©Raphael Reischuk / pixelio.de

More available books at **www.hansebooks.com**

A

MEMORIAL

OF

NATHAN B. CROCKER, D.D.,

LATE RECTOR OF SAINT JOHN'S CHURCH,

PROVIDENCE, R.I.

EDITED BY

RICHARD B. DUANE.

RECTOR.

Providence:

SIDNEY S. RIDER AND BROTHER.

1866.

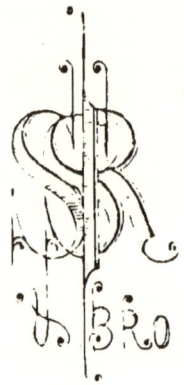

CAMBRIDGE:

PRESS OF JOHN WILSON AND SON

SERMON

PREACHED IN

SAINT JOHN'S CHURCH, PROVIDENCE,

ON

Sunday, October 29, 1865,

BY THE

REV. RICHARD B. DUANE, RECTOR.

At a meeting of the Vestry of Saint John's Church, Providence, on the 30th October, 1865, the following resolution was adopted: —

Resolved, That the Rev. Mr. DUANE be requested to furnish for publication a copy of the Discourse delivered by him yesterday, in commemoration of the life and services of our late Rector; and that he be respectfully invited to add to it such biographical or historical notes as he may deem of interest or value.

SERMON.

"And they glorified GOD in me." — GALATIANS, i. 24.

THIS is the testimony of an inspired apostle. It is his testimony in regard to a matter of fact. It is made with all meekness and lowliness, yet in such a way as to show that the meekness and lowliness were by no means recognized on the part of the writer. With simplicity and godly sincerity, he merely says that "the churches of Judea, which were in CHRIST," glorified GOD in him, — that is, gave thanks to GOD on account of him ; praised GOD for his conversion ; praised GOD for the work which he was doing who now preached the faith which he once destroyed.

The fact which St. Paul here records is no less eminently Christian than the way in which he delivers the statement of it.

When those early simple-hearted Christians heard of St. Paul, and that he who had once been a persecutor and injurious was now a chosen vessel in which the LORD was bearing about the Gospel, they did not glorify the apostle; they did not enumerate, with churchly pride, the gifts and powers of this well-furnished ambassador of CHRIST: but they praised GOD for it all. And this is the more striking when we remember, that St. Paul, in natural endowments and in all advantages for culture, stood so much higher than the other apostles of the LORD. The account of his conversion excited them to adore the grace of GOD towards him, and to bless Him for raising up so useful a minister of His word.

As I attempt to-day the duty which the death of our late beloved friend and Rector brings to me, I wish at once to place before you the example of these Judean Christians. It is worthy of imitation. We are to glorify

GOD in him who, for so many years, minis-
tered to you in holy things. We are to thank
GOD for his work and service who preached
so long the faith which he had before, at least
negatively, destroyed. This is our first duty;
a duty, I fear, sometimes entirely overlooked,
when our memorial sermons are mere pane-
gyrics, good in themselves, but not rising
above that which is of the earth, earthy, —
not taking into consideration the LORD from
heaven, who is also the "LORD of all power
and might." For all natural endowments, all
gracious influences, all opportunities of usefulness, are equally the gift of one and the
self-same SAVIOUR.

Our late Rector was born while as yet the
clouds of our Revolutionary War hung over
the land. We thus get at the long reach
of life which was granted him. When he
first saw the light, on the fifth anniversary of
the nation's birthday, Cornwallis was being
pursued by Lafayette near the James River;
while the French under Rochambeau, and the
Americans under Washington, were threaten-
ing Clinton in New York. The curious in

such matters will notice with interest, that, as the day of his birth was the anniversary of the day when our independence was declared, so the day of his death was the anniversary of the day when that independence was secured. He lived to see that other great struggle for Liberty and Union through which we have just passed, to sympathize in its vicissitudes, to rejoice in its success and its results. It was a long life that touched both these wars.

Born in Massachusetts, he pursued his academic and collegiate course in that commonwealth; and, soon after he reached his twenty-first birthday, began the study of medicine in Portsmouth, N.H. In the autumn of the same year, he came to Boston, intending there to continue his studies. It was at this juncture that God's guiding hand was particularly laid upon him. He was accustomed to speak of the circumstance as the work of Him who was even then leading the blind by a way that he knew not.

The physician upon whom he called, and under whose instructions he proposed to place himself, was ill, — too ill to be seen. Young Mr. Crocker then came to the town of Providence to tarry a while, until Dr. Jeffries should recover. While here, he was asked to fill the position of lay-reader in St. John's, for which his rich and delightful voice might have pointed him out as suitable, and which he accepted, as he himself expressed it, with "mingled emotions of gratitude and diffidence." He continued here, persuaded by friends to pursue his studies for the ministry. Even before his ordination, he was elected to be Rector as soon as he obtained Deacons Orders; and, in May, 1803, he was duly established over the flock. This office he assumed for one year, signifying his "cheerful acceptance of the arduous and important office." So feeble, however, were his bodily powers at this time, and so great was the disability arising from an affection of the eyes, that twice during the year he obtained leave of absence; the second leave being extended to the close of the twelvemonth for which he had accepted his place. During the ensuing three years, he was for some time abroad;

although he occasionally visited, and preached to, his former charge. In the spring of 1807, a committee of the parish was appointed to open communication with him. He returned, resumed his labors, and from that time went no more out, until the LORD' opened the door of Paradise, and bid his blood-washed soul enter into blessedness. During the earlier years of his Priesthood, the building in which we now worship was erected.

In the year 1815, there occurred the great change in his own heart, which was nothing more or less than a passing "from death unto life," a new creation in JESUS CHRIST. When Mr. Crocker took upon him the great responsibilities of the sacred office, he was actuated by no base motives. He intended to do his duty. But, as he afterwards well knew and confessed, he was practically a stranger to the life-giving power of the Gospel. He had, indeed, erected an altar; but it was an altar to an unknown Christ. His preaching was consequently devoid of the marrow of the Gospel. It was serious, sober, — in some sense, perhaps earnest; and it was enforced by a life which had been always correct and unblamable before men.   But —

> " Oft, when Paul had served him with a text,
> Had Epictetus, Plato, Tully, preached."

The LORD had better things in store for him and for this congregation.   One day, while in a bookstore, he took up a volume of President Edwards's works.   It was that upon " The History of Redemption."   For such writings Mr. Crocker had no relish.   I might with truth use a stronger term than this.   He was prejudiced against the man and his writings. Casually, as men say, he opened the book, and read a few sentences.   The HOLY SPIRIT accompanied the truth to his soul.   He was riveted; he was enchained.   He bought the book, took it home with him, and devoured its contents.   Henceforth he was a new creature: old things had passed away; all things had become new.   His conversion was decided.   Like St. Paul, " he straightway preached CHRIST."   At this period, as is now generally agreed, there was, in the Church at large, great deadness, great ignorance, great opposition to the truth as it is in JESUS. Hence it is not to be wondered at, that the new doctrines stirred up some to be opposers. Wherever there is "a great door and effectual opened," there will be "many adversaries." The opposition here was so decided, that Mr. Crocker was taken to task in his vestry-room by two members of the congregation. His doctrines were strongly objected to, especially the doctrines of the corruption of the human heart and of Divine retributions. He replied by opening the Bible, and silencing the objectors with the words of Holy Writ. This occurred on Sunday, the 23d July, 1815. On the next Sunday morning, with unusual solemnity and emphasis, he preached from the text, "I *determined* not to know any thing among you, save JESUS CHRIST and Him crucified." As one records in a manuscript dated that day, "Mr. Crocker's manner, when he first commenced the service, was uncommonly solemn, particularly when he repeated, 'Let the words of my mouth and the meditation of my heart be alway acceptable in thy sight, O LORD, my strength and my Redeemer.'

The words of the text were repeated without mentioning either chapter or verse. He rose and said, 'For I am determined not to know any thing among you, save JESUS CHRIST and Him crucified.' . . . He told his congregation that the Sun of Righteousness had not yet risen among them with healing on his wings; spoke of their being angry with their minister; told them the ministers of CHRIST meant no self-exaltation when they preached the truth to their people, but it was the great concern they felt for their souls. . . . One part of his sermon was like a prayer. . . . Our Rector, instead of offering an apology to his congregation for preaching in a way to offend them the Sunday previous, made use of several of the same expressions which he did in the sermon that was the cause of so much noise and disturbance."

The effect of such preaching of the Gospel in a valley of dry bones may be imagined. The LORD blessed the work of his servant; and, at the next Convention, he reported forty-six persons added to the communion. From that day until he no more

officiated, he "ceased not to teach and preach
JESUS CHRIST."

Let us glorify GOD in him. What an awful contrast would have been presented in his
own soul, in this parish, in this city, if the
Blessed Spirit had not shined into his heart
fifty years ago, to give him the light of the
knowledge of the glory of GOD in the face
of JESUS CHRIST! And this contrast would
not have ceased at our confines. The position of this parish, so near to a seat of learning like Brown University, has given an
influence for good with many of its students;
and more than twenty young men, who became in this parish communicants of the
Church, entered the ministry.

It is to be regretted, that, during the ten
years which succeeded Mr. Crocker's entrance
upon the ministry, there were no parochial reports published in the Convention journals.
The history of the ministry of our late Rector,
for seven years, is thus devoid of data which
are attainable. During the fifty years beginning with 1813, the following are the ministerial acts performed by him: He baptized over

eleven hundred individuals, of whom seven
hundred and fifty were infants; he admitted
about six hundred and fifty persons to the
Holy Communion; he officiated at nearly three
hundred and fifty marriages, and at more
than five hundred and fifty funerals. The
number of communicants rose from fifty-nine
to two hundred and thirty-eight in the same
period, the parish having been twice instrumental in establishing a new parish from
within itself. During all this period, he
was remarkably stable in his religious views,
and steadfast in the proclamation of "the unsearchable riches of CHRIST." In Cowper's
words, —

> "I would express him simple, grave, sincere;
> In doctrine uncorrupt; in language plain,
> And plain in manner; decent, solemn, chaste,
> And natural in gesture; much impressed
> Himself, as conscious of his awful charge,
> And anxious mainly that the flock he feeds
> May feel it too; affectionate in look,
> And tender in address, as well becomes
> A messenger of grace to guilty men."

As one expresses it, "A theologian of varied
acquirements and of positive views, and a

Churchman warmly attached to his particular Church, he was at all times kindly and
catholic in his tone. . . . Such has been the
career of this venerated Christian minister,
as it has been witnessed and honored by two
entire generations of this community. It was
quiet and industrious, unostentatious and unambitious; it borrowed no advantage from
station or ecclesiastical preferment; it was
marked by no factitious brilliancy, such as
sometimes gathers its ephemeral halo around
even a clergyman : but it was illumined, from
beginning to end, with the mild radiance which
always comes from a pure character and a
consecrated life."

Dr. Crocker's reports at the Convention
were sometimes very characteristic. Thus he
says in 1842 : "GOD, in his good providence,
continues to prosper St. John's Church. He
gives us peace among ourselves, preserves us
from extremes, and vouchsafes that steadiness
of moral growth which so uniformly charac-
terizes his own works." In 1844, he says:
"By the grace of GOD, the members of St.
John's Church dwell together in unity, and

still hold fast to the old orthodoxy of the Reformation. This will at all times be matter of gratitude. But, in these days, that which will give most pleasure to a Christian mind is the fact, — perhaps I had better say my own conviction, — that a spirit of unaffected piety, a feeling of the infinite importance, to themselves and others, of the Gospel, as communicating pardon and salvation in the person and grace of a Divine Saviour, — in some good measure, pervade the communion." In these words are mirrored the mind of this anxious pastor. He was jealous with a godly jealousy over his people, "that the truth of the Gospel might continue with you." It was this which led him to be one of the founders of the Evangelical Knowledge Society, and to approve of the purposes and work of the Episcopal Missionary Association for the West, and of the American Church Missionary Society. The Gospel, which he loved and preached, he would have had everywhere spread abroad, with nothing to mar in the least its simplicity, fulness, and freeness. This led him to be active in missionary work in the Convocation of this Diocese, and to be a warm advocate of foreign missions. He rejoiced that CHRIST was preached. He had himself passed from darkness to light, and had experienced the power and preciousness of Divine truth.

In closing these allusions to the spirit and work of our late revered Rector, I mention two characteristics.

The first, which pertained to his personal character, was a devout recognition of the special, over-ruling providence of GOD. He had been too carefully taught in that school to fail in profiting by the repeated lessons. A hymn from the German of Paul Gerhardt * was a very great favorite with him, —

> "Be thou content; be still before
>   His face at whose right hand doth reign
> Fulness of joy for evermore, —
>   Without whom all thy toils are vain.
> He is thy living spring, thy sun, whose rays
> Make glad with life and light thy weary days.
>   Be thou content.
>
> "We know for us a rest remains
>   When GOD will give us sweet release

---

* Lyra Germanica : Fifteenth Sunday after Trinity.

> From earth and all our mortal chains,
>   And turn our sufferings into peace.
> Sooner or later, death will surely come
> To end our sorrows, and to take us home.
>   Be thou content."

The second, which pertained to his ministerial character, was his implicit reliance upon the grace of the HOLY SPIRIT for success in the work of winning souls to CHRIST. This is well illustrated in his own words, written in 1844: "The great object of our labor is the glory of GOD in the conversion of sinners; and, while we would not forget to seek the edification of the Church, and can never fail to find a pleasure in it, nothing can make the Christian's heart so glad as to hear men honestly and earnestly inquiring what they must do to be saved. . . . From what was the congregation a year ago, only nine have been added. That many, nevertheless, will come, and from present appearances we cannot but think ere long, is as certain as the Scriptures of truth can make it, if the Gospel is preached in humble dependence upon the unseen but omnipotent power of the SPIRIT."

Thus with faith he waited, in the day when the harvest was small, for a brighter and a better day; and GOD rewarded his faith.

These two characteristics are but the outgrowth of the inner Christian life which the LORD implanted in him, and for which we glorify GOD in him. Whether in providence or in grace, he "set the LORD always before him." He depended on the TRIUNE JEHOVAH for guidance, for pardon, for cleansing, for a blessing on his ministry. As the book of hymns which hung upon the wall of his study was turned on last Monday morning to the twenty-third day, the hymn there printed was "Rock of Ages," which had already been selected to be sung at the solemn funeral hour. It was a happy coincidence, and shadowed forth the ground of our dear Rector's hope and trust.

The closing years of this man of God were spent in retirement, alike grateful to his body and his mind. He was not devoid of all suffering; but, in a great degree (as one of our parishioners remarked to me), the petitions of the special prayer, which we offered every

Sunday afternoon, were heard and answered. He was "delivered from bodily pains, and his soul kept clear and serene, so that no cloud ever came between him and his Saviour." While he spoke latterly of the "labor and sorrow" which are so generally the portion of him who "comes to fourscore years," he regarded the past few years as a period especially blessed in the opportunities for personal growth in grace. That those opportunities were improved, they understand who have taken knowledge of his deep and unfeigned contrition, his abiding trust in Jesus, his desire for spiritual blessings. In the last interview I was permitted to enjoy with him on earth, all these came richly forth as the evidences of a soul ready to go to be with Christ. And I may be permitted to add, that the Lord, in continuing his life as Rector among you, after the days of active effort were passed, conferred a benefit upon yourselves, some of the fruits of which I think I see, and more of which I hope to see.

When we look back over the long period during which he served in this place, what

thronging memories arise! Few linger in
these seats who were here when he began
his work. What numbers have been born,
have come to this house of prayer, have
listened to his voice, and have gone before
him into the unseen world! What tender
memories are associated with his name and
person! Here has he taken to his arms the
little babe, to enroll him among the people of
the LORD. Here has he united hand with
hand, as they clasped in token of vows of fond
affection. Here has he stood to witness, in
Confirmation, the dedication of numbers to the
cause of CHRIST. Here has he given the sacred symbols of a SAVIOUR's Body and Blood,
with the prayer that all who thus partook might
indeed be partakers of CHRIST. Here has he
conducted those solemn rites prepared for the
burial of the dead which were lately used for
him. He is associated, and has been for long
years, with the tenderest, the most solemn, occasions in the lives of most of you.

He sleeps. He sleeps in JESUS. He has
followed many to whom he taught the way
of life, and is, as they are, with CHRIST.

We are irresistibly drawn in our thoughts to that day of the LORD's appearing when the trumpet shall sound, and the dead shall be raised incorruptible. In that day of overwhelming and awful joy to CHRIST's people, quick and dead, "the LORD JESUS shall be revealed from heaven," "to be glorified in his saints." Our beloved brother in CHRIST shall arise to everlasting life. The spiritual children whom GOD gave him shall arise to everlasting life. If, in your day, the LORD shall come, then ye Christians, who are the seals of his ministry, shall be caught up together with them to meet the LORD in air; and so shall all ever be with the LORD. This re-union of pastor and people, of spiritual father and spiritual children, in the glorious presence of Him who was and is and ever shall be "all and in all," — who can speak of it aright? Shall you, my friend, be among that blood-bought and blood-cleansed throng? May the HOLY SPIRIT press the thought upon you, until, in the confidence of a certain faith, in the comfort of a reasonable, religious, and holy hope, and in the communion of the

Catholic Church, you can humbly answer, "LORD, thou knowest all things; thou knowest that I love thee"!

BIOGRAPHICAL SKETCH.

BIOGRAPHICAL SKETCH.

———

NATHAN BOURNE CROCKER, son of Ebenezer and Mary (Bourne) Crocker, was born in Barnstable, Mass., on July 4, 1781. The Crockers were of Cotuit, and the Bournes of Sandwich, both in Barnstable County. Young Mr. Crocker fitted for college at the academy in Sandwich, and was graduated at Harvard College on the 25th of August, 1802.*

Soon after his graduation, he began the study of medicine with Dr. Leonard, of Portsmouth, N.H.; and afterwards came to Boston, intending to place himself under the direction

---

* From an account of Christ Church, Gardiner, Me., prepared some years ago by the Hon. R. H. Gardiner, the following extract is taken: "In July, 1802, the parish engaged Mr. N. B. Crocker, who had just graduated, to read prayers for three months."

of Dr. Jeffries. The doctor being too ill to be seen, Mr. Crocker came to Providence, in company with the Rev. Nathaniel Bowen, at that time the youthful Rector of St. John's, Providence, and afterwards Bishop of South Carolina. They arrived on the 22d of October. On the 24th of October, Mr. Bowen preached his farewell sermon, having served the parish about ten months; and, on the 28th, departed, to become Rector of St. Michael's Church, Charleston, S.C. On the 31st of the same month, Mr. Crocker commenced his duties as lay-reader in St. John's. On the 11th of April, 1803, he was "elected to be Rector as soon as he obtains Deacon's Orders." The person who was chiefly instrumental in persuading him to study for Holy Orders was Mr. John Innes Clarke, a parishioner. From a manuscript still existing, it appears that he did not become a communicant until Feb. 20, 1803, when he "partook of the sacrament for the first time." His parents were Congregationalists; and the time of his baptism, and that of his becoming an Episcopalian, are alike unknown.

Mr. Crocker received Deacon's Orders at the
hands of Bishop Edward Bass, of Massachusetts, in Trinity Church, Boston, on the 24th of
May, 1803. This was within a few months
of the Bishop's death. At this period, the
Rev. Messrs. Dehon (consecrated Bishop of
South Carolina in 1812) and Crocker were
the only Episcopal clergymen in Rhode Isl-
and. There were only four parishes in the
diocese. Providence was a commercial town
of six or seven thousand inhabitants, an'd
contained six houses of worship. St. John's
(formerly King's) Church had been standing
eighty years.

Mr. Crocker's first sermon in his parish
was preached on the 5th of June, 1803, from
St. Luke's Gospel, fifteenth chapter, sixth and
seventh verses. During the earlier part of his
ministry, his health was so feeble, that, twice
during the year 1803, he obtained leave of
absence from his parish. The second leave
was continued until the year was closed
for which he had accepted his office; viz.,
until May 24, 1804. Owing to the state
of his health, he embarked for Lisbon, on

June 7. Although Mr. Crocker did not re-
sume the duties of the Rectorship for nearly
three years, yet he preached from time to
time to his former congregation. In the autumn of 1804, he preached for six weeks,
and again preached in March, 1805. The
Rev. John L. Blackburn officiated from December, 1805, until March, 1807. Upon his
leaving the parish, a committee was at once
appointed to write to Mr. Crocker, with a
view to his resuming the Rectorship. He
arrived in Providence in April, and commenced his duties on the 26th; accepted the
Rectorship early in the following year (to
date from the time of his receiving Priest's
Orders); and was ordained Priest on the
18th of May, 1808, by Bishop Benjamin
Moore, in Trinity Church, New York. From
that time until his death, he continued to be
the Rector; thus serving in one church for
nearly sixty years.

In the year 1810, Mr. Crocker was married
to Eliza Antoinette, daughter of Dr. Isaac
Senter, of Newport. Three of their four children survived their parents.

In June, 1810, the corner-stone of the new church was laid, and the church consecrated in June, 1811.

After the change in Mr. Crocker's religious views, in the year 1815, his preaching became very popular, especially attracting the students at Brown University, even those who were not religious young men. His new-born zeal led him to missionary effort; and he was probably the first home-missionary of our Church in New England. This soon resulted in the establishment of the parish at Pawtucket, called "St. Paul's, North Providence." In missionary work, carried on in after-years by the Convocation of Rhode Island, he was particularly interested and engaged.

From 1808 until the year of his death, with the exception of one year, Dr. Crocker was a member of the Standing Committee of the Diocese, and, for a long time, its President. He was elected a delegate to nineteen Triennial General Conventions. He received the degree of Doctor of Divinity in 1827, from Geneva College. He was a Fellow of Brown University from 1808, and, for fifteen years,

Secretary of the College Corporation. For the seven years before his death, he was the oldest Presbyter of the Episcopal Church in the United States.

Dr. Crocker was three times proposed for Bishop of the Diocese,—in 1843, in 1853, and in 1854. In 1853, there was no election, the clerical vote being equally divided; and, the year following, he was nominated by the clergy, but the nomination was not confirmed by the laity.

Dr. Crocker was assisted in the duties of the parish by various clergymen during the last ten years of his ministry, — by the Reverends Lucius W. Bancroft, Legh R. Dickinson, Horatio Gray, Charles H. Wheeler, James I. T. Coolidge, and Richard B. Duane.

His last sermon was preached on the 16th of June, 1861, from Romans viii. 31, —"If GOD be for us, who can be against us?" He administered the Holy Communion for the last time on Easter Day, April 20, 1862.

He fell asleep in Jesus on the 19th of October, 1865, aged eighty-four years. The funeral services took place on the 23d, in St. John's Church ; and his body was laid at rest in the North Burying Ground.

Clergymen who confessed Christ for the first time in our Communion at St. John's : —

* EVAN M. JOHNSON, D.D.
* THOMAS CARLILE.
* JOHN L. BLAKE, D.D.
* GIDEON W. OLNEY.
  ALEXANDER JONES, D.D.
* JASPER ADAMS, D.D.
  GEORGE TAFT, D.D.
  EDWARD R. LIPPITT.
  SAMUEL B. SHAW, D.D.
  JOSEPH MUENSCHER, D.D.
  D. L. B. GOODWIN.
  ETHAN ALLEN.
  SILAS A. CRANE, D.D.
* CHARLES DRESSER.
* HENRY B. GOODWIN.
* The Rt. Rev. GEORGE BURGESS, D.D.
* JAMES W. COOKE.
  NICOLAS HOPPIN, D.D.
  THOMAS L. RANDOLPH.
  NICHOLAS P. TILLINGHAST.
  SAMUEL COWELL.
  RICHARD C. HALL.
  T. STAFFORD DROWNE, DD., — 22.

Mr. GEORGE B. PAINE died in 1858, on the eve of Ordination.

---

* Deceased.

Clergymen who were connected at one time (generally in early life) with St. John's as parishioners, but who afterwards confessed Christ for the first time in our Communion in another parish:—

    * WILLIAM RICHMOND.

       THOMAS S. W. MOTT.

       JOSEPH S. COVELL.

       ALEXANDER H. VINTON, D.D.

       FRANCIS VINTON, D.D.

       ELEAZAR M. P. WELLS, D.D.

       HENRY WATERMAN, D.D.

    * JAMES C. RICHMOND.

    * ROBERT NORTHAM.

       ALEXANDER BURGESS.

    * J. WARD SIMMONS.

       EDWARD L. DROWN.

       McW. B. NOYES.

       J. STURGIS PEARCE.

* Deceased.

Clergymen who, having united with our Communion else-where, were, while in Providence, connected with St. John's Church as parishioners: —

The Rt. Rev. BENJAMIN B. SMITH, D.D.
* GEORGE GRISWOLD.
* BENJAMIN C. CUTLER, D.D.
JOSEPH H. PRICE, D.D.
M. A. D'W. HOWE, D.D.
* EPHRAIM MONROE.
FRANCIS PECK.
GEORGE D. MILES.
ANDREW MACKIE.
HORATIO GRAY.
LUCIUS W. BANCROFT, D.D.
F. MARION McALLISTER, — 12.

NOTE. — Reminiscences from a number of the clergy-men mentioned in these lists, will be found in the succeed-ing " Correspondence."

* Deceased.

CORRESPONDENCE.

CORRESPONDENCE.

November 22, 1865.

REV. AND DEAR BROTHER, —

It gives me great pleasure to furnish such reminiscences as occur to me in relation to one from whose hands I received my first communion, and who was for many years my faithful pastor, and the friend of my youthful days. During the first few years of Dr. Crocker's ministry, his sermons, like those of most of the Episcopal clergy at that time, partook more of the character of moral essays than of evangelical discourses. They were ethical, rather than doctrinal and experimental. They were chaste, rhetorical, and ornate; abounding, as he sometimes expressed

it, in "picks and posies," — very pleasant to
hear, but producing no deep and lasting
impression.   But a happy change in this respect was in store for him ; and he was
destined to occupy a far more elevated and
useful position, as an ambassador of CHRIST,
than he then did.   Some time in the fall or
winter of 1812, I believe, the Rev. J. P. K.
Henshaw, afterwards the Bishop of your Diocese, was ordained a Deacon in St. Michael's
Church, Bristol, R.I., on which occasion
Dr. Crocker was present.   The sermon was
preached by the Rev. John Kewley, in which
he faithfully delineated the duties and responsibilities of the Christian ministry.   This
sermon, I was informed, made a very deep
impression on Dr. Crocker's mind, and led
him to regard the subject in a very different
light from what he had heretofore viewed it.
Of course, a corresponding change took place
in his preaching, which became much more
solemn and impressive.   In February, 1813,
I purchased a copy of Scott's "Family Bible.'
Dr. Crocker made a parochial call on my
mother just at that time, and, seeing the work

on the table, asked the loan of the first volume, which he retained in his possession some
six months.   He perused it with deep interest;
and I have reason to believe that it was instrumental, to a great extent, in giving that
tone and complexion to his theological views
which ever after characterized them.

I became a communicant of his Church in
August, 1813.   At that time, the male communicants properly belonging to his Church,
including myself, numbered only seven; and
I was the only young person among them.

In the summer of 1814, the subject of a
weekly meeting for prayer and religious im-
provement was suggested.   For satisfactory
reasons, Dr. Crocker declined to attend the
proposed meetings; but expressed his hearty
approval of the measure, and encouraged us
to go on.   The first meeting was accord-
ingly held in a private house.   The exercises
consisted of prayer, partly precomposed and
partly extemporaneous; singing; reading of
the Scriptures, and of some printed sermon.
The attendance at first was small, but soon
increased; and a deep interest was felt in

them by all the more serious and devout members of the Church and congregation. They continued to be held regularly, in private houses, till 1817, when, in consequence of the large attendance, they were removed to the court-house. As soon as this removal took place, or soon after, Dr. Crocker took charge of the meetings.

During the years 1814 and 1815, I took pretty copious notes of the Doctor's sermons; and find, on recurring to them, that he preaches with great fidelity and pungency, but apparently with but little success. Something was necessary to arouse the public conscience, and quicken the pulsations of spiritual life. This want was soon supplied. On Sunday, July 23, 1815, the Doctor preached a very searching discourse from Ps. lxxiii. 19, "How are they brought into desolation as in a moment!" He described the condition of impenitent sinners in terms calculated to arouse the latent enmity of the unrenewed heart to God, and to awaken deep concern and alarm in the minds of thoughtful inquirers. The congregation, generally, was not prepared for

such an outspoken exhibition of the terror of
the LORD, and it caused no little commotion
and disturbance among many of his hearers.
Two prominent members of the congregation
called on Dr. Crocker to expostulate with him
on the character of his recent sermons generally, and particularly of the one just referred
to. The faithful and fearless pastor is reported to have said, "Ought I to be dictated
to by two or three gentlemen in the choice of
my texts ; on what subjects I shall preach, and
how I shall discuss them?" They replied,
"Most certainly not." — "How then, gentlemen," he rejoined, "am I to understand your
present visit?" While they disclaimed any
intention of dictating to him on these points,
they still insisted that the sermon before
alluded to was highly objectionable both in
sentiment and expression. On inquiring of
them what there was in that sermon which
was particularly offensive, they referred him
to the following sentence : "The bow of GOD's
wrath against the wicked is bent, and the
arrow made ready on the string. Justice
points the arrow to their breasts, and nothing

but the restraining hand of God prevents it
from piercing their hearts." The Doctor in-
stantly opened his Bible, and, turning to Ps.
vii. 11–13, showed them, that, in employing
the bold, figurative language of which they
complained, he had simply expressed the sentiment of the psalmist, and quoted almost
literally his very words.

On the following Sunday, the Doctor
preached in the morning from 1 Cor. ii. 2,
—"For I determined not to know any thing
among you, save JESUS CHRIST and Him
crucified;" and, in the afternoon, from 1 Cor.
iii. 5–7, —"Who then is Paul, and who is
Apollos, but ministers by whom ye believed?"
&c. These sermons were kindly in tone, but
manifested great firmness and decision of purpose as to what ought and might be expected
from him in the discharge of his duty as a
dispenser of the blessed Gospel of the grace
of God. The voice of opposition was soon
hushed; the sympathy of true Christians,
irrespective of denominational distinctions, became warmly enlisted in his behalf; and addi-
tions began to be made rapidly both to his

congregation and communion. It was the opening of a brighter day on that Church than she had ever experienced during the long period of her previous existence.

Though far removed from the scenes of my early life, my memory often travels back to the time when I listened, with deep interest, to the discourses of Dr. Crocker; and never without emotions of unmingled satisfaction and gratitude to GOD for permitting me, in His providence, to sit for years, during the forming period of my life, under the faithful ministrations of one so skilful in dividing the Word of Truth, and so faithful in dispensing it to those committed to his charge.

Very truly, I am your friend and brother in CHRIST,

JOSEPH MUENSCHER.

Rev. RICHARD B. DUANE.

November, 1865.

REV. AND DEAR BROTHER, —

During the last two years and a half of my college course, I found myself identified with all the work and interests of St. John's Church; at a period in its history, and of the ministry of its then comparatively young Rector, as memorable as ever marked the history of a strong parish, or of a transformed and ennobled life.

As I look back upon those days, I am at once conscious of the difficulty of separating the most powerful emotions of my own inner life, just then for the first time sensitively if not fully alive to the things of GOD, from the external realities with which I was surrounded; my religious exercises, from my religious teaching; the influence of our sublime Liturgy upon my imagination and my heart, from the effect of a fine voice and excellent manner in rendering it; and of Divine truth, enforced with passionate earnestness in the first clear perception of it, and the fresh experience of its life-giving power. At that time, I was by no means a judge of the solid merits of a preacher : but, as my memory now serves me by the light of the experience of riper years, I should say that Dr. Crocker, at that time, was not a doctrinal or logical preacher, nor particularly full or instructive ; but he was eminently practical, and intensely in earnest. How far the fruits of his ministry were to be traced to its characteristic merits, I should be entirely unfitted to determine ; since the whole period, to my mind, seems so filled with a Divine influence. The entire congregation, with very few exceptions, seemed so famishing for the bread of life, that truth from any source was what they wanted, and the lessons of religious experience, and the instructions of duty ; and these his Divine Master had just taught his docile disciple. His heart was full of them ; and, when he preached, the Divine fountain overflowed.

Sunday-School work, Tract-Society work, and every healthy form of parish work, soon gave evidence of the sincerity of the many converts who filled St. John's during that

favored period; and, if I mistake not, many
of the fruits remain until this day, and, for
years to come, will render fragrant the memory of Dr. Crocker.

I am, yours faithfully,

B. B. Smith.

———◆———

November 18, 1865.

Rev. and dear Brother, —

My first religious impressions were received
and nurtured, and my views of Divine truth
were imbibed and greatly moulded, under the
ministry of the Rev. Dr. Crocker; and I look
back to my connection with St. John's Church
with the liveliest emotions of interest and
gratitude to God, whose gracious providence
placed me, at this period of my life, under
the influence and guidance of so faithful and
earnest a servant of our Divine Master.

It had not been long before this period, that
his own mind had been led, under the Holy
Spirit's teaching, to a wider and more just
comprehension of the vital truths of the Gos-

pel, and to a deeper and livelier interest in his
own salvation, and that of the large flock
committed to his charge. The fundamental
truths of Revelation — such as the fall and
corruption of man; the necessity of conversion; justification by faith only; and good
works, the fruit and evidence of saving faith
— were dwelt upon with a constancy, distinct-
ness, and fulness in the pulpit becoming these
vital doctrines; and with an earnestness, fresh-
ness, and eloquence which aroused the attention, and forced their way to the intellect and
heart, of his people. As a consequence result-
ing from this faithful preaching of the Gospel,
and in accordance with the promise of the
Great Head of the Church, a very general
spirit of inquiry was awakened in regard to
the evangelical doctrines of the Bible, the realities of eternity, and the salvation of the
soul. In the height of this excitement and interest, it is believed that there was scarcely an
individual among the large attendance on his
ministry who was not moved by the Divine
Spirit that so evidently accompanied the exhibition of Divine truth. The accession to the

communion during a period of many months, at each sacramental season, was large.

Time and space will permit me to illustrate these general statements by furnishing a description of a single scene. It had been determined to hold a night-service in the church, for the first time, on Christmas Eve. What a strange and violent prejudice even then (1815) existed against such a service! but which, not long after, passed away; never again, it is hoped, to return. So intense was the interest, what with the gratification of curiosity and better motives, the streets leading to the church, some two hours before the time of service, were alive with people wending their way to the novel and strange sight of St. John's opened after night for Divine worship. Before the commencement of the service, the house was so densely filled and closely packed, pews and aisles, that there was no room for another; and hundreds were disappointed in gaining entrance beyond the vestibule. After the reading of the service by the pastor, in his own earnest and impressive manner, he ascended the pulpit with a counte-

nance and gait which bespoke how solemnly
and deeply he felt the responsibility of address-
ing such a large gathering of dying sinners
hastening to a bar of judgment. He an-
nounced for his text our SAVIOUR's answer to
the woman of Samaria, recorded in St. John's
Gospel, chapter fourth, and verse tenth, — "If
thou knewest the gift of GOD, and who it is
that saith unto thee Give me to drink, thou
wouldst have asked of Him, and He would
have given thee living water." The stillness
of death pervaded the church during the delivery, for nearly an hour, of the sermon prepared for the occasion, and admirably adapted
to the character of the large and promiscuous
assemblage. Many an arrow of conviction
did it convey to the conscience, and many an
emotion of fear and anxiety did it excite in
the breasts of the audience, — indicated by the
bowed head and falling tear, — and which, ere-
long, ripened into firm resolve and open con-
fession of CHRIST. It is known to the writer,
that not less than a dozen persons, under the
influence of that sermon, and before they left
the sanctuary, passed the crisis of their re-

7

ligious history, in determining to take their
stand on the LORD's side. Eternity alone will
disclose the momentous results of this first
night-service in St. John's Church, on Christmas Eve, 1815.

Yours, in the best of bonds,

E. R. LIPPITT.

The Rev. R. B. DUANE.

————◆————

November, 1865.

REV. AND DEAR SIR, —

I commenced attending on Dr. Crocker's
ministry in September, 1818, when he was in
the prime of his manhood, and not long after
he had attained those clear views of Gospel
truth which he so decidedly maintained to
the end of his life. I had been accustomed
to hear sound and earnest divines; but the
preaching of Dr. Crocker, at that period, was
enlightening and impressive to a remarkable
degree. His very appearance in the pulpit
was striking and attractive; his form tall,
graceful, and erect; his voice remarkably

clear and musical; his enunciation distinct;
his language invariably choice and elegant;
his pronunciation a standard of correctness;
and his whole delivery, while restrained within
the bounds of strict propriety, was earnest and
engaging to such a degree, that none but the
utterly indifferent failed to be interested and
awakened, and made sensible of their personal interest in the truths presented. And
(as a history of the parish at that time would
show) not more admirable was the preaching
than salutary its effect upon the numerous
congregation. "Many believers were added
to the LORD." And not only were they out-
wardly and visibly connected with the LORD's
people, but they were eminently "of one heart
and one mind;" they "loved as brethren, were
pitiful, were courteous."

The Doctor's sermons, for the most part,
were freshly written; for he was peculiarly
loath to preach a sermon a second time to his
congregation. The range of his subjects was
wide and diversified; and, except the interviews which he held with individuals previous
to baptism or confirmation, there seemed to be

less need of personal oversight than in the case of most other parish ministers.

I am sincerely yours,

D. Le B. Goodwin.

The Rev. R. B. Duane.

———◆——

January 8, 1866.

My dear Mr. Duane,—

I knew Dr. Crocker from my earliest recollection, and loved him always; but my first and very strong impression of him dates from a period of religious excitement in St. John's Church about the year 1816. I was but a boy; but I remember distinctly the agitation in the parish at the sudden change in the manner of his preaching, and in his whole ministerial course.

The account which he gave me, in subsequent years, of this critical period in the history of the parish and of himself, was substantially like this:—

Having entered the ministry with no very deep views of its responsibility, and with a theological training shaped from the pattern of a low Arminianism, he had a natural impatience of every form of Calvinistic doctrine, and an especial dislike towards the name and memory of Jonathan Edwards as the great apostle of the system. On one occasion, at a bookstore, he took down a volume of Edwards's works from the shelf with a sort of half-malicious curiosity, and in order to gather material for fresh dislike. The volume chanced to contain the "History of Redemption." He opened it at hazard, and found his attention so fastened, that he stood reading for a long while, unconscious of the lapse of time. At length he bethought himself that it was long past his dinner hour; but, unwilling to part with his book, he bought the whole set, and took them home with him, reading without intermission till he had finished the volume on Redemption. He rose from his task possessed and overpowered by the conviction that he had known nothing hitherto of the Gospel of Salvation, and had lived a mistaken life. With this conviction began a revolution in his religious life, which he was accustomed to speak of as a conversion; and, with it, an entire change in his style of preaching.

It could hardly be expected that so sudden a transition, from mild and meagre sermonizing to pungent and awakening exhibitions of Divine truth in its most startling aspect, should fall without effect upon a congregation bred in the traditional indifferentism of Queen Anne's times. The dull ear was pained, and the unwilling heart stirred to repugnance; and, for a time, the parish was disturbed by the antagonism of the friends and opposers of the new system.

On one occasion, the Rector was waited upon in the vestry-room by two leading laymen of the Church, as a committee to remonstrate and protest against the new doctrines, and the peculiar language in which they were presented from the pulpit. The Rector vindicated his phraseology as being the language of Scripture; and, upon this fact being disputed by the gentlemen, he took them at once to the desk, and showed them in the Church Bible the very language which they deemed so obnoxious, and which he had only quoted.

They were silenced, of course; and, as Dr. Crocker expressed it, completely amazed.

A religious awakening followed this change in his style of ministration, and St. John's Church became, in the course of a few years, eminent among the churches for its devoted attachment to Evangelical principles, and for the liberal fruits of the Evangelical spirit in all good words and works : an eminence which it has maintained to this day.

The theology which Dr. Crocker had thus adopted was, of course, Calvinism in its decided, though I believe not its extreme form. He always held prominently, practically, and implicitly the doctrine of the Divine Sovereignty, and went forward in his ministrations contented to pray and wait for the fruits of his labors whenever it should please GOD to send the harvest; and he never waited in vain. The blessing always seemed to come periodically, and without special preparation or effort on the part of the minister, or through any habitual or direct personal influence, for which Dr. Crocker was not eminently adapted; but as the legitimate result of earnest Evangelical preaching, the sure honor with which GOD crowns his truth.

I am yours, very truly,

ALEX. H. VINTON.

————◆————

November 13, 1865.

MY DEAR BROTHER, —

My acquaintance with our venerable friend, Dr. Crocker, began while I was a student in Brown University. Previous to that, I had known nothing of the Episcopal Church; and I entertain no doubt that his very impressive manner of reading our Liturgy did much to make me feel and appreciate its beauty and excellence, and thus to turn my attention to the claims of the Church in other respects. Subsequently, I became a member of his Church, and pursued my theological studies under his pastoral and friendly care. I was presented for confirmation, by Dr. Crocker, in St. John's Church; and not a few of the most important events, as well as the sweetest memories, of my life have been long tenderly associated with that Church and its venerated Rector.

His character, as a faithful preacher of a blood-bought and finished salvation, is too well known in all the churches to need or to receive any commendation from me or from any man. The last sermon which I heard him preach was delivered in my own Church. It was marked by all the doctrinal clearness and vigor of his earlier days; and, at the same time, seemed to me to be, more than any other discourse I had ever before heard from him, distinguished by tenderness and love for the souls of men, and an outflowing of his heart with the words of his mouth, which gave unmistakable evidence, that, as he advanced in age, he was growing more and more into the true spirit of the blessed JESUS. My last interview with him was in July of this year. I was then much affected with the meekness and gentleness of his spirit; the extreme kindliness of feeling with which he spoke of persons and occurrences connected with the history of his ministry; and specially with

8

the calm trust in which he was prepared to
enter into the dark valley of the shadow of
death, and to render to the final JUDGE an
account of his stewardship. "GOD," said he,
"is dealing very gently with me, and letting
me down step by step." His work was done
in respect to others. He was then trimming
his own lamp to be ready for the call.

Very truly your friend and brother,

S. A. CRANE.

———◆———

November 10, 1865.

MY DEAR MR. DUANE, —

When Dr. Crocker was in his best strength,
suppose in 1830, he was, in manner, aspect,
and doctrine, such a representative of his
Church as could not but engage a most re-
spectful attention. To me, from childhood,
all associations connected with our communion and ritual had him as their central figure ;
and I have sometimes wondered how far these
early memories would have possessed the same
beautiful and solemn sanctity had another held

his place. As he rose in the desk, or stood in the chancel, his very tall, erect, and slender form, so elegant in all its remarkable proportions; the priestly dignity with which he moved in his surplice; the spectacles, always worn; the exact clerical propriety of his garb; and then the matchless intonations of his voice as he read the Litany with so much fervor, — all so accorded with the very character of the venerated service itself, that no years can remove the union between it and him in one delightful remembrance.

A very marked solemnity appeared to me, in my youth, to characterize the sermons of Dr. Crocker, as well as his manner in the pulpit. There could be no misapprehension of the great subjects of his preaching, — the deep corruption of fallen nature, salvation through the atoning SAVIOUR alone, and then the work of the HOLY GHOST. If, sometimes, he seemed severe in the denunciation of sin, or confined in the circle of his topics, the hearer still felt the healthful, bracing power of clear doctrine brought home to the conscience.

It was thus, and through the dignity of his own character, that Dr. Crocker exercised, through a course of years of service almost unparalleled amongst us, the power not only of binding together a parish of very large influence, and of adding constantly to the number of its spiritual ornaments, but also that of drawing a high order of young men towards the ministry. Other divines have been more ready in debate, and more copious in conversation: nor was he a silent man; but, without words, he could often lead more effectually and farther than those whose social or public eloquence seemed most commanding.

Since his age and infirmities withdrew him from his active labors, I have, from time to time, enjoyed a short visit to his study. He spoke with a most cheering pleasure of the opportunity which his retirement afforded him for more peaceful meditation, for some reading for which he had lacked time, and for seasons of precious devotion. In one of the very last of our interviews, he told me, almost in the identical words which Bishop Brownell,

at the same age, had used to me a few
months before, that he had never been happier
than now.

Blessed old man! the beloved and faithful
pastor of successive generations. How has
his noble congregation honored itself by cling-
ing to him to the end of his sixty years! He
is gone to those who loved him, and were led
by him in green pastures, and beside the still
waters. While I think of them as now with
him again, my heart and my eyes gush over.

Affectionately your friend and brother,

GEORGE BURGESS.

———◆———

November 18, 1865.

REV. AND DEAR SIR, —

It is gratifying to pay my slight tribute to
the many high qualities of the late revered
Rector of St. John's.

The long period in which his hoary head
was a crown of glory in the way of righteousness does not prevent my recalling him as
vividly when the raven-black of his luxuriant

hair was yet scarcely sprinkled with gray.
For the last thirty years I have been a com-
parative stranger in my native city, and have
only on rare occasions met with Dr. Crocker;
but the memories of early life are sufficient
for a character so fixed. To the youthful eye,
he was already the impersonation of sacred
dignity; a quality which advancing years
might blend and soften, but could scarcely increase. It was never absent, never less; and
the impression of it was even deepened by his
occasional brief but well-chosen and sufficient
words of kindness to the young, and the un-
failing courtesy of his recognition. It would
be hard to say which in him was most
marked, the polished gentleman or the consecrated minister of GOD. That he was distinct-
ively either, never caused it to be forgotten
that he was eminently the other.

But the reverence which Dr. Crocker inspired, grew mainly out of a feeling that
Divine truth, which it was his office to teach,
entered deeply into his own inner life, and
gave the character to his outward manner.
Though averse to making religion the topic of

general or promiscuous conversation, it was
evidently never far off from his thoughts;
and, when the right occasions came up, especially for private counsel or instruction, they
were not lost. Many have been struck with
the direct frankness with which he would, at
such times, go straight to the point, and, as it
were, take the trembling hand and lead a
hesitating believer to CHRIST, or a doubtful
inquirer to the very best action under the
peculiar circumstances. There was, too, a
blunt honesty of advice, always sensible and
discreet, which surprised the more as coming
from one of such extreme courteousness, mingled ordinarily with not a little reserve.

In writing hastily, two special traits of Dr.
Crocker, as I have known him, recur prominently, — steady laboriousness and thoughtful
kindness. I remember the patient and minute
fidelity with which he would go through long
portions of the sacred books, by way of expo-
sition, in weekly lectures, courses of which
would sometimes be given on Sunday even-
ings, in addition to the morning and afternoon
services and sermons, which were never short

nor slighted. This love of the Holy Scriptures, and desire to have them known and
loved, seemed to make him forget weariness,
and to find refreshment in the task.

Instances of personal kindness, unsolicited,
thoughtful, seasonable, unexpectedly repeated
once and again, will not be forgotten; and
they are also in the record, made up on high,
of multiplied offerings by a willing people
under his prompting and guidance.

With sincere respect, I am, very truly,
yours,

NICOLAS HOPPIN.

—◆—

November 20, 1865.

REV. AND DEAR BROTHER, —

The decease of Dr. Crocker, though antici-
pated from his advanced age and increasing
infirmities, awakens all the feelings of a personal loss. Accustomed in early life to look
up to him as my pastor and friend, memory
has been busy with the pleasant interviews
and acts of kindness of former years; and I
realize now, even more deeply than ever be-

fore; the debt of gratitude which I owe him. Receiving from his hands the rite of baptism, admitted at his chancel to my first Communion, enjoying his faithful and instructive ministrations during my college life, and becoming a candidate for the sacred ministry under his affectionate advice and encouragement, I came to respect and love him as a spiritual father.

During the period of our more intimate acquaintance, there were no incidents, that I now recall, peculiar or unusual enough to be of public interest. The character and tastes of the man would make this almost impossible. Not only were the duties of his profession all quiet and unobtrusive of themselves, but he always had a decided repugnance to any personal notoriety or sensation whatever. He studiously kept himself in the background, best contented and pleased if he could but give all prominence to the name, and make attractive the example, of his Blessed Master. Well-balanced as was his mind, — with no marked peculiarities, except it were an unshaken love and an unflinching advocacy of what he believed to be the "old and good way," and an equally undisguised detestation of all novelties or extravagances, whether in doctrine or ritual; finding his whole time and powers occupied in the usual round of pastoral duties, — the events of his life were the words spoken and the services rendered in the Church and by the hearth-stone, in the sick chamber and by the open grave. Whatever he said or did was always marked by the thoughtfulness and courtesy of the Christian gentleman, and the winning and earnest affection of the faithful pastor. Nothing could be more charming than an interview in his quiet study, in the old residence in College Street, years ago, where, surrounded by his well-used books, and kindling with unwonted animation over some prevailing error or ecclesiastical question of the day, he poured out a rich tide of learning and wisdom; or, if some private doubt or grief had prompted the call, exerted himself, with all the solicitude and tenderness of a father, to clear up the difficulty or assuage the sorrow. In his public discourses, of which he must have prepared a vast number during so long a ministry, —"always writing," as he once told me, "one, and often two, every week,"— he seemed to aim invariably at the best good of the hearer; avoiding all dogmatism, and ever advocating, with a clear enunciation, and a persuasive earnestness peculiarly his own, what was thoroughly practical and evangelical. Few will ever forget the impressive manner, and the rich, full tones with which he used to read the lessons and prayers of the Church, or pronounce the solemn office for the burial of the dead.

Looking back upon his life as I remember it, what impressed me most was his devout and tranquil cast of character. Upheld by a firm and unquestioning trust in Providence, resting his all upon the anchor within the veil, the agitations and vicissitudes of the world had little power to disturb his wonted composure. This spirit dwelt within through all the trials and changes of a prolonged life; an undecaying lamp, burning without flicker or dimness, trimmed and fed by daily prayer and meditation, and shedding a radiant and serene light upon all who came within its influence.

But his name is now only a memory! He
rests from his labors, and his works do follow
him. No one among the living can estimate
the influence, or sum up the usefulness, of a
life and an example like his. Already aged
when most of us were young, his teachings
and efforts have contributed no little towards
moulding the minds and hearts of two generations. Not only will his name and virtues be
preserved as a precious tablet in the Church
on earth, but in the last day, when every
man's work shall be made manifest, many
will they be who shall rise up and call him
blessed.

Very sincerely yours,

T. STAFFORD DROWNE.

—◆—

November 29, 1865.

MY DEAR AND REV. BROTHER, —

A lady, who was a teacher in St. John's
Sunday School while I was superintendent,
has lately sent me the following interesting
statement of some remarks made by Dr.

Crocker at a meeting of the Sunday-School teachers of St. John's, while she herself was connected with that delightful circle : —

"I remember one occasion in my youth when I saw more of Dr. Crocker's inner life than I ever did at any other time. It was at a meeting of the Sunday-school teachers of St. John's, that he was speaking of the great change which first brings a man to the knowledge of himself and of his SAVIOUR. He said that, in his own case, this change took place instantaneously, while he was reading a volume of Edwards's works; that he went into Mr. Johnson's bookstore, — the old shop which then stood opposite the First Baptist Church, — and that, without previous intention or any particular interest in its contents, he took up the book, and began to read it; that he *stood* reading without fatigue, forgetting surrounding circumstances, absorbed and enchained and melted, until he was roused to the consciousness of time and place by finding the tears pouring down his cheeks. He said it was the day of his conversion, and that a new life dawned on him from that hour. The fervor and tenderness with which he described the sudden emerging of his soul from darkness to light were very remarkable ; and the habitual absence of reference to himself and his own emotions in conversation made the unreserve of this personal narrative still more striking."

Affectionately yours,

N. P. TILLINGHAST.

———◆———

December 28, 1865.

REV. AND DEAR SIR, —

I became connected with the Sunday School of St. John's Church, as superintendent, in the spring of 1824. At that time, I think there were about forty scholars, who met in a room on Canal Street. In a conference with Dr. Crocker, soon after my acceptance, he asked with earnestness, "What can I do to promote the interests of the school?" I remarked to him, that a feeling appeared to prevail, not only amongst ourselves but throughout the community, that Sunday Schools were intended only for the poorer classes, and that, until that impression was removed, we could not expect much increase. It seemed to be a new idea to him. After a few moments, he said, "That is too true, and this false notion must be removed. I will preach a sermon on the subject," — which he soon did, and a capital sermon it was; in which he set forth the importance, as well as the benefits of a religious training of children, and the duty of parents, in whatever situation of life, to see that their children availed themselves of every means that would promote the object. That one of these means, and an important one, was the Sunday School. Towards the close of his sermon, he said, with much emphasis, "What others may do I know not; but this I know, that my children shall attend the school." It produced a wonderful effect; and, in a very short time, nearly all the children of the parish were members of the school, and we soon numbered over one hundred and fifty scholars. Our example was followed by others in the city; and this change of feeling was, in a great measure, owing to the influence and example of Dr. Crocker. No school was ever blessed with a more devoted and able corps of teachers than we were; and we were always readily and cheerfully sustained by Dr. Crocker in every good word and work. We had only to make our wants known, to have them promptly and cheerfully supplied. So far as I am informed, the first library, as well as the first Infant School, was established by St. John's.

Very truly yours,

GEO. S. WARDWELL.

S E L E C T I O N S.

10

SELECTIONS.

EXTRACTS FROM A SERMON

Preached in Grace Church, by the Rt. Rev. Thomas M. Clark, D.D.. Bishop of the Diocese, on Sunday evening, Nov. 5, 1865.

The Protestant Episcopal Church in this country had been organized only twelve years when Mr. Crocker read service for the first time in St. John's; and his name appears upon the journal as a member of the Rhode-Island Diocesan Convention, in 1807. It was a day of small things in the Church, so far as numbers were concerned; for the only clerical delegate besides himself in that Convention was the Rev. Theodore Dehon, Rector of Trinity Church, Newport, and who, like the

clergyman whose place Dr. Crocker had occupied five years before as lay reader, afterwards became Bishop of South Carolina.

The professional life of the late Rector of
St. John's is intimately connected with the
growth of our Church in this Diocese. When
he came here, there were but four Episcopal
churches in Rhode Island; all of them established under the auspices of the British Society
for Propagating the Gospel in the early part
of the last century. Of the statistics of the
Diocese, we have no record till the year 1813,
when it appears "that there were one hundred
and forty-eight communicants in Bristol, one
hundred and five in Newport, and fifty-nine in
Providence." No report is made by the church
in Kingston. The four churches, planted a
century and a half ago, had not seen one new
parish added to their number until 1816, when
St. Paul's Church, Pawtucket, was received
into union with the Convention. The Rev.
Mr. Crocker, having become imbued with the
missionary spirit, a species of feeling that was
somewhat rare in those days, had been sometimes in the habit of travelling out to Paw-

tucket, when his Sunday labors were over, to hold service in the evening; and this good work of his was crowned with the Divine blessing. It was the first work of the kind, so far as I am informed, that was ever done in New England after we became an independent Church. He was the original Episcopal domestic missionary in this section of the country. The venerable man who in youth took charge of this parish still lives; but the weariness of age is weighing heavily upon him, and he has for the most part ceased to discharge the public duties of the ministry.

.   .   .   .

Of his personal traits, it is hardly necessary that I should speak in this community. His appearance was such as would attract attention everywhere: tall, erect, and manly in person, courteous and dignified in his bearing, a single glance served to show that he was a true gentleman. Somewhat reserved in his manners, he never repelled you by any thing approaching arrogance. Positive in his opinions, strong in his prepossessions, he was singularly kind and forbearing, as all will testify who knew him. I think I never knew a man more utterly devoid of personal ambition. He shrank from every thing tending to attract public attention to himself. He more than once expressed a strong desire, which we have been constrained to disregard, that nothing should be said in public, regarding him, after his decease.

. . . .

The closing years of Dr. Crocker's life were full of tranquillity and peace. He had his days of suffering and his nights of weariness, and he often longed for the hour when he should depart, and be with JESUS; but he always felt that he was in the hands of One whose chastisements were those of a father, and he bowed meekly to the rod. When free from pain, his spirits rebounded with singular elasticity, and he would express the highest sense of enjoyment. His religion was of a peculiarly devotional type; and in this fact he found great comfort, when no refuge remained but the Cross of CHRIST. Under the shadow of that Cross he could lie content while the life-strings were giving way, and the world was receding from his view. To recall familiar passages of Scripture and holy song furnished all the intellectual solace that he needed; and, the more often they were repeated, the greater seemed to be their charm.

At last he rests from his labors. The stately form which has long been familiar to us all, which many of you remember from your earliest childhood, will be seen no more moving through our streets. The gentle voice which has often reminded you of your duty, and entreated you to make your peace with GOD, will be heard no more on earth. The spotless life, whose example preached more eloquently than words, has ended.

———◆———

EXTRACT FROM A SERMON

Preached in St. Stephen's Church, on Sunday, Oct. 29, 1865, by the Rev. HENRY WATERMAN, D.D. : —

. . . WE have been led into these reflections (brethren), by that solemnity of Monday last at which some of you were present, and in which the honored patriarch of our

Church in Rhode Island was borne, amid the
soothing offices of the Church, to the last
and most peaceful of his slumbers. At the
" full age " of fourscore and four years,
the late Rector of St. John's Church has
gone, we cannot doubt, to a blessed repose,
accompanied by the affectionate prayers and
farewells of his beloved flock, and by grateful
regards and pleasant memories on the part of
a whole community. As we recall the last
few years of his life, and especially the occasions on which we met his emaciated form in
the street, moving with bent shoulders, — with
that slow and feeble tread, and with that staff
in his hand, — have we not thought, sometimes, at least, how good it was to look on
the whitened locks of an aged pilgrim of
CHRIST, of whom we felt that a few steps
more would bring him to his home, where
every thing would be safe and sinless for ever?
His own thought was, perhaps, that he had
outlived the days of his usefulness : but,
apart from the general truth, so full of conso-
lation, that —

" They also serve, who only stand and wait,"

I can believe, and *do* believe, that his old age itself was a silent preacher; that, from a character which old age had ripened and mellowed, there went abroad a quiet but healing grace, which will be found, in the records on high, not to have gone forth in vain.

Seven weeks ago to-morrow, I saw, for the last time, the form of the venerable Rector. He had invited a few of his clerical brethren to meet him at his bedside, and "show forth" a SAVIOUR's death. His soul was refreshed, in that chamber of suffering, by the dear Sacrament of our redemption, the Eucharistic bread and cup which his hands had stretched out so many times to others at the chancel-rail. In the strength of that heavenly nourishment, he crossed the dark river.

It would be eminently fitting for us to pause, and take note of any providence which should remove, from a sister parish in the same city, its priestly head, its spiritual father and guide; but the providence which appeals to us this morning has had for me, as it must have had for some of you, an especial interest.

More than eight and thirty years ago, being
then a lad at school in this city, I entered, one
Sunday morning, St. John's Church. It was
the first Episcopal Church I had ever been in;
and its Rector was the first Episcopal clergyman whom I had ever seen officiating in the
sanctuary. The worship of the Church was
as great a novelty to me as can well be imagined. But the impressions made upon me
that day have remained with me until this day.
I look back with gratitude upon that Sunday
as one of the epochs of my religious history.
You will not, therefore, be surprised that I
cherish pleasing recollections of that sanctuary
and of its late pastor, as associated with blessings to which they were the instruments of in-
troducing me; and you can excuse, I am sure,
the seeming egotism in these references to the
past. And now that the good pastor is gone,
I can but give GOD thanks, now and here, in
others' behalf as well as my own, for all the
good conveyed to us through that servant of
CHRIST. . . .

[The following is from the "Providence Daily Journal" of Tuesday, Oct. 24, 1865.]

REV. DR. CROCKER.

THE death of this venerable minister of the gospel naturally awakens a deep interest throughout the community in which, for so long a time, he has been a conspicuous citizen. We cannot but recur again to an event which has been so widely felt by all classes of our people. His funeral took place yesterday, with impressive rites, at eleven o'clock, at St. John's Church, where, more than sixty years ago, he began to preach the gospel. And, in the service of one and the same Church, from the beginning to the end, he has passed his entire professional life, fulfilling the relations and performing the offices of a Christian pastor to the same people, longer, probably, than any other minister in the generation to which he belonged. His tall and erect figure, which scarcely bent beneath the burdens of increasing age, his dignified and genial manners; his clear and richly toned voice, his Christian kindness and worth, his integrity as a citizen, and his services as a faithful pastor, have been familiar to the people of Providence for so long a period, that very few now among us can remember when they were not here. They will long be enshrined in the memory, not only of his immediate parishioners, but of the whole community. All feel that a revered patriarch has been taken away, that a pure and useful life has been brought to a serene and happy close, and that the most venerable human form that walked our streets has faded for ever from our view.

His life has been one of singular uniformity and stability, and has been quietly devoted to the faithful and unostentatious performance of his duties as a parish clergyman. We can recall no other instance of a minister of the gospel spending upwards of sixty years in the parish in which he was ordained, and dying, at the age of eighty-four, still the pastor of the same congregation to which he preached his first sermon. Without question, and as a matter of course, he still retained the place to which he had been called by an earlier generation, and was cherished with reverence and affection by the children and the children's children of those with whom his ministry began. This fact, so far as we know, stands alone in recent ecclesiastical history; and, in this day of fluctuating tastes and opinions, it reflects the highest credit alike upon pastor and people. Equally stable was he in his principles and his modes of presenting them. A theologian of varied acquirements and of positive views, and a Churchman warmly attached to his peculiar Church, he was also, at all times, kindly and catholic in his tone; and made it his aim to preach, not the peculiarities of a sect, but the essential truths of the gospel. Others changed in their estimates of what is most important; portions of the general Church to which he belonged put forth new views and adopted new usages, —but he did not change. As he was in the maturity of his manhood, so was he to the end of his life, — a plain and faithful preacher of the doctrines of Repentance and Faith.

For a considerable period, Dr. Crocker had
been the senior Presbyter of the Episcopal
Church in the United States; and, up to 1859,
he had attended, as a delegate, every one of
its triennial conventions which had been held
during fifty years. He was long a member of
its Board of Missions, a councillor and gov-
ernor in its seminaries of theological educa-
tion, and was also the founder of several of
the parishes of that communion which have
sprung up in this State since he was settled in
Providence. Nor did he ever stand aloof
from the religious or social interests of the
community, but always delighted to unite
with good men of every persuasion in pro-
moting the progress of knowledge and virtue
and piety. He had been for fifty-seven years
a member of the Board of Fellows of Brown
University, and was thus connected with the
government and care of the University longer
by far than any other person whose name is
recorded in its history. In recognition of this
fact, and more especially in testimony of the
high respect entertained for his personal character, he was requested in the summer of

1860, as he was entering upon his eightieth
year, to sit for his portrait, to be placed in
Rhode-Island Hall; the cost of which was
defrayed by the contribution of a fixed sum
from some ten or twelve hundred of his fellow-
citizens. The work was executed by Mr.
Huntington of New York, and is one of the
best portraits in the interesting collection gathered at the College.

Such has been the career of this venerated
Christian minister, as it has been witnessed
and honored by two entire generations of this
community. It was quiet and industrious, unostentatious and unambitious. It borrowed no
advantages from station or ecclesiastical preferment. It was marked by no factitious brilliancy such as sometimes gathers its ephemeral
halo around even a clergyman; but it was illumined, from beginning to end, with the mild
radiance which always comes from a pure
character and a consecrated life, from an integrity that temptation does not overcome, and
a piety that grows brighter through the lapse
of years. It was the career of one whom all
unite in honoring as a faithful servant of God.

[Minute entered upon the Records of the Vestry of St. John's Church at a meeting held on Oct. 30, 1865.]

THE Rev. NATHAN BOURNE CROCKER, D.D., Rector of this parish for nearly sixty years, — viz., from 1803 to 1804, and from 1807 to 1865, — departed this life at his residence in this city on Thursday evening, Oct. 19, in the eighty-fifth year of his age.

The Vestry desire to place on record an expression of their gratitude to Almighty GOD, that He graciously gave to this parish, for so many years, the clear example and the pure teachings of one whom He "called by His grace," and "in whom He had revealed His SON."

They desire to commemorate their late Rector's faithfulness in preaching "the glorious gospel of the Blessed GOD," his missionary spirit, and his faith in the Divine Word as accompanied by the influences of the HOLY GHOST.

They would bear in mind, and transmit on these pages, the excellence of his personal character and the value of his ministrations: and they would cherish his memory as of one who has finished his course, and kept the faith, and for whom there is "laid up a crown of righteousness, which the LORD, the Righteous JUDGE, shall give him at that day."

At the same meeting, the following resolutions were adopted: —

Resolved, That a Committee be appointed, to whom shall be intrusted the duty of obtaining a plan for a commemorative monument; said Committee to report at a future meeting of this body.

Resolved, That the Clerk of the Vestry be requested to transmit to the family of our late Rector a copy of the above Minute and Resolution.

———◆———

[Extract from the Records of the Quarterly Meeting of Convocation held at St. Thomas's Church, Greenville, Nov. 2, 1865.]

Rev. Dr. Waterman and Rev. Mr. Duane, a Committee to prepare Resolutions relative to the death of Rev. N. B. Crocker, D.D., late

Rector of St. John's Church, Providence, reported the following, which were unanimously adopted by a rising vote : —

Forasmuch as it hath pleased Almighty GOD, in His wise providence, to take out of this world the soul of our deceased brother, the Rev. N. B. Crocker, D.D, for nearly sixty years Rector of St. John's Church, Providence, this Convocation desire to enter upon their records their sense of the value of the labors of one who, in the early years of missionary work in this diocese, and for a long period, was untiring in his efforts for the establishment of the Church.

They would transmit on the records of this body this memorial of the personal worth, and long and diligent ministry, of their departed brother in the LORD.

Resolved, That copies of the foregoing be sent to the family of the deceased, and to the Vestry of St. John's Church.

[Resolutions adopted by the Board of Missions, Oct. 20, 1865.]

WHEREAS, The Board of Missions have received tidings of the decease of the Rev. Nathan Bourne Crocker, D.D., Rector of St. John's Church, Providence, a distinguished and one of the earliest of the members of this Board, and eminent for his long and devoted Rectorship of sixty years; therefore —

Resolved, That the Board of Missions recall with gratitude the pure example of piety, gentleness, and fidelity to his holy calling, of the Rev. Dr. Crocker; and, in thus expressing their reverence for his memory, would tender to the friends and the congregation of their deceased friend their unfeigned sympathy for the great grief of their bereavement.

[Preamble and Resolution adopted in the House of Clerical and Lay Deputies in General Convention, Oct. 21, 1865.]

WHEREAS, This House has heard of the death, during the present session, of the Rev. N. B. Crocker, D.D., for the last seven years the oldest Presbyter of the Protestant Episcopal Church in the United States; for the unprecedented period of sixty years the respected Rector of St. John's Church, Providence, in the Diocese of Rhode Island; and from that time, until the infirmities of age prevented his attendance, an honored member of every successive General Convention; therefore —

Resolved, That this House feels it a duty to enter on its Journal a grateful memory of, and respect for, this beloved brother and faithful servant of the Lord JESUS.

[Extract from the Address of Bishop Clark to the Diocesan Convention, June 12, 1866.]

DURING the session of the General Convention, that venerable man whose name has been identified with the history of this Diocese for two whole generations, and who had survived every clergyman and layman who sat with him in council more than half a century ago, the Senior Presbyter of our American Church, breathed his last, and was gathered to his fathers. It is not necessary, in this presence, that I should attempt an elaborate portraiture of the Rev. Dr. Crocker's character, or pronounce his eulogy. As far back as any of you can remember, he stood as a sentinel on the towers of Zion, loyal and vigilant, his whole heart and soul concentrated in the work which his MASTER had given him to do. The one object in which all his efforts centred was the winning souls to CHRIST. His faith never faltered; his zeal never abated; his love never grew faint; his piety, like his life, was placid and uniform. With him there were

no startling scintillations, alternating with pe-
riods of darkness; but he shone like a steady
light on the shore, that burns on, all through
the night, without change or intermission.　It
is sad to think that we shall see his venerable
form no more, and never hear again his calm
voice in our councils.　He was the leading
man in this Diocese before most of us were
born.　For a time he was almost the only clergyman resident here.　We read his name in
the Journal of 1808, and from that time it has
been called in this Convention every year until
the present.　It will be heard here no longer;
but we doubt not that it was found written in
the Book of Life, and has already been heard
in paradise.

———◆———

[Resolution of the Diocesan Convention, June 13, 1866.]

Resolved, That, as members of this Convention, we cordially respond to the Right
Reverend, the Bishop of the Diocese, in the
very appropriate remarks which he yesterday
made in his Address touching the decease and

character of two of our clerical brethren, who were for many years associated with us, and bore an active and honorable part in the labors and counsels of this ecclesiastical body, — the late venerable Rector of St. John's, in this city, the Rev. Nathan Bourne Crocker, D.D., and the late Rector of St. James's, Woonsocket, the Rev. Baylies P. Talbot : and that, while we cherish with respect and affection the memory of their pure and exalted Christian characters, and of their example as faithful ministers of CHRIST, we also desire hereby to make a public and permanent record in our Journal of the esteem and affectionate regard in which these our brethren were held among us.

—◆—

[At a meeting of the Corporation of Brown University, on the morning of Sept. 6, 1860, the following communication was received from the Committee whose names are appended to it : —]

To the Corporation of Brown University.

IN the month of May last, a few gentlemen of this city met, by common agreement, for the purpose of considering in what manner there might be appropriately expressed to Rev. Nathan B. Crocker, D.D., the venerable Rector of St. John's Church, the high respect and esteem in which his character and services have long been held by his fellow-citizens of Providence. The gentlemen thus meeting were not connected with Dr. Crocker by ecclesiastical associations; and their only object was to devise a suitable mode of giving expression to what they well knew to be the common sentiment among all classes of the community. At this meeting, it was determined to request Dr. Crocker to sit for his portrait, to be executed by some artist of distinction, and to be placed, when finished, with the consent of the corporation, in Rhode-Island Hall, with the other portraits belonging to the University. At the same time, the undersigned were appointed a committee to carry this determination into immediate execution. In order to give as general a character as practicable to the proceeding, it was also decided to fix the subscriptions for accomplishing the purpose at the uniform rate of one dollar for each person.

In accordance with the general idea thus indicated, the undersigned have performed the grateful duty which was assigned to them. Immediately on obtaining the consent of Dr. Crocker, they engaged the services of Mr. Daniel Huntington of New York, an artist of high reputation in this department of his art. They also set on foot, in different portions of the community, the subscriptions which were required for defraying the expense. The portrait has now been executed by Mr. Huntington with eminent success. It possesses not only great fidelity to the form and features it was designed to portray, but also superior excellence as a work of art; and it will not fail to commend itself, to those who may look upon it, as a beautiful specimen of artistic execution.

The entire professional life of Dr. Crocker has been spent among the people of Providence. In an age that has been filled with changes, it has been distinguished for its uniform and unambitious fidelity; and it strikingly illustrates the happy results of permanence and stability in the relations of a Christian minister to the community in which his lot is cast. He was born in Barnstable, Mass., July 4, 1781. He graduated at Harvard College in 1802; and, in October of the same year, he came to Providence, and conducted public worship in St. John's Church as Lay Reader until the following May, when he was ordained a Deacon in the Episcopal Church. In June, 1804,* he was ordained a Presbyter; and soon afterwards was instituted as Rector of the parish of St. John's, the office in which he has continued to the present time. He is now the oldest clergyman of the Protestant Episcopal Church of the United States; and, for more than fifty years, he has been a member of each of its triennial conventions, excepting only the last. At Commencement in 1808, he was elected a member of the Board of Fellows of Brown University; a post which he still continues to fill, and which has connected him with the government and care of the University for a longer period than any other person, whether living or dead, whose name is recorded in its

* This is an error. The date should be May 18, 1808.

annals. Within this period, he has also been secretary of the Corporation fifteen years, and a member of the library committee more than sixteen years. This briefest outline of his long career, extending through nearly two generations, will suggest to every mind the services which constitute his pre-eminent title to the gratitude and honor both of this city and the University.

Having now fulfilled the purpose for which we were appointed, it only remains that we present the work with whose execution we have been intrusted, to the body for whose custody it was originally designed. We therefore respectfully request the Corporation to accept this portrait for the University, in behalf of the numerous subscribers whose names are herewith communicated, as a token of the respect and esteem which are cherished for this venerable gentleman by his fellow-citizens in Providence and its vicinity. It is designed to be a testimonial to his pure life and worthy example; to the fidelity and usefulness of his life-long services among us as a minister of the gospel; and to the sympathy which he has always manifested with the well-being, both moral and social, of this community. We ask that this portrait may be suspended with those already collected in Rhode-Island Hall; and we earnestly hope that it may remind the scholars of the University, and all who in the present or in future time shall gaze upon it, how beautiful and venerable is a serene and unostentatious life spent in the performance of elevated duties and in labors for others' good.

In behalf of those for whom we have acted, we have the honor to remain, very respectfully,

JOHN KINGSBURY.
WM. S. PATTEN.
JOHN R. BARTLETT.
WILLIAM GAMMELL.
SAMUEL G. ARNOLD.

PROVIDENCE, Sept. 4, 1860.

[The foregoing communication having been read and accepted, the following Preamble and Resolutions were adopted : —]

WHEREAS, as appears by the foregoing communication, there has been presented to this University, in the name and behalf of a large number of the people of Providence and its vicinity, a well-executed portrait of Rev. Nathan Bourne Crocker, D.D., as a tribute of the respect and esteem which are cherished for his character and services as a Christian minister and as a man during his long residence in this city ; it is therefore —

Resolved, That we, the members of the Corporation, gratefully accept this valuable work of art; and that we delight to recognize it as a tribute of respect for one who, during a period of fifty-two years, has been intimately connected with us and our predecessors in the councils of the University.

Resolved, That we honor the sentiments which have prompted the people of Providence and its vicinity thus to express their grateful appreciation of the character and life of this venerable minister of the gospel; and that, in placing his portrait in Rhode-Island Hall, they have most fittingly indicated the relations which he has so long sustained alike to the city and the University.

A Mural Tablet is to be placed in the Church bearing the following inscription :—

En Memory
OF
THE REVEREND
NATHAN BOURNE CROCKER, D.D.,

Who within these walls preached
"the unsearchable riches of Christ"
for nearly sixty years.
He served in St. John's Parish as
a Lay Reader in the year 1802;
and as Rector, in the Diaconate and Priesthood,
in 1803-4, and from 1807 to 1865.
He entered into his rest, Oct. 19, 1865;
aged 84 years.
Graced with a commanding person,
a saintly countenance,
a voice of peculiar melody,
and a truly reverent manner,
He conducted the worship of the Sanctuary
with deep solemnity
and most impressive effect.

A PASTOR
refined in manners,
sympathetic in spirit,
and wise in counsel;

A PREACHER
sound in doctrine,
simple and lucid in style,
earnest and persuasive in delivery.

HIS PARISH,
served for fifty years by him alone,
prospered throughout his Ministry.
Beloved by his own Flock,
revered by all,
He turned many to righteousness.
His memory is precious upon Earth,
and his reward great in Heaven.

www.ingramcontent.com/pod-product-compliance
Lightning Source LLC
Chambersburg PA
CBHW032150010726
47493CB00008BA/2645